The Crazy Man

The Crazy Man

PAMELA PORTER

GROUNDWOOD BOOKS
HOUSE OF ANANSI PRESS
TORONTO BERKELEY

Groundwood Books / House of Anansi Press
110 Spadina Avenue, Suite 801, Toronto, ON M5V 2K4

Distributed in the USA by Publishers Group West
1700 Fourth Street, Berkeley, CA 94710

We acknowledge for their financial support of our publishing
program the Canada Council for the Arts, the Government of
Canada through the Book Publishing Industry Development
Program (BPIDP) and the Ontario Arts Council.

ONTARIO ARTS COUNCIL
CONSEIL DES ARTS DE L'ONTARIO

Library and Archives Canada Cataloguing in Publication

Porter, Pamela Paige.
The crazy man / by Pamela Porter
ISBN-13: 978-0-88899-694-7 (bound).–
ISBN-10: 0-88899-694-2 (bound).–
ISBN-13: 978-0-88899-695-4 (pbk.)–
ISBN-10: 0-88899-695-0 (pbk.)
I. Title.
PS 8581.O7573C73 2005   jC813'.6   C2005-903001-1

Printed and bound in Canada
Design by Michael Solomon
Cover illustration by Karine Daisay

For Rob, Cecilia and Drew,
who love that great, flat land
with its enormous sky

Emaline

HALF THE TOWN'S DRIVING PAST OUR FARM
today, churning up dust on the road
just to stare at a man
driving a tractor.

I've gone upstairs to my room.
Going to try to figure out
this whole big mess.

The Saskatchewan sun's pouring down
in a bright rectangle
on my floor, and dust
is dancing in the sunlight.

I'm making a new mark on the wall
behind a corner of my mattress, hidden
so only I know it's there
with all the other pencil lines.
Every four crossed catty-cornered
to make five.

My arm gets tired and lets the mattress slip.
But I got it counted.

        Thirty-two days since that day
my daddy dragged Prince's body to the burn pile
and set it afire,
then walked away from the farm.
And us.

THAT DAY BUILT A ROOM INSIDE MY HEAD
where we all live — Daddy, Prince, Mum and me.
I want to build a door for that room
                              so I can shut it off,
and if I think about it real hard, maybe
I can build that door.
Because that day's living in my brain now,
and it's all colored red.

There's me, walking home from Haig School
at the very end of April, nineteen sixty-five.
Our first hot spell. At the edge of town
I have to pass the mental hospital
                              which looks like a castle
behind a long line of caragana bushes
towering way over my head.

Joey and Jamie, twins from down the road,
they run past that place every time. But me,
I don't mind it. I just imagine
I'm in England — me, Emaline Bitterman —
and the queen lives there,
and I walk by, calm as a cabbage.

Then my feet hit the dirt road
and our white house is there and Prince
barks and runs up, and I hear our tractor
running in the field behind our house. And I see
Dad's discing the field.

Well, I drop everything
and run up to that tractor and hop on.
When Dad works the fields,
                              I like to ride
standing right behind the seat.

So I do. And I'm smelling the churned-up
dirt, and I'm feeling the spring breeze
with a promise of summer in it,

and all of a sudden Prince
starts chasing a big snowshoe hare
that's run out of its hole
from the noise and rumble
of the tractor. That hare's scooting
                              zig-zaggy in fear,
and it's running right where the discer's coming.

And Prince isn't watching
the discer either. He's after that hare
and he's chasing that hare
right into the discer.

And I'm scared that Prince
will get his paws cut off in the discs
and I yell, "Prince!"
and jump off the back of the tractor
                              to save him.

And my foot lands right in front of the end disc.

Then everything gets fuzzy.
Dad's yelling and Prince
is barking and somehow
                    Mum's there
and my foot's dangling
below my leg — red foot,
red leg, red dirt.

And now I remember
Dad, Prince, the tractor,
everything,
in red.

I DREAMT ABOUT PRINCE,
his hot breath in my ear.
The prairie wind blowing my hair.

I lay on my back on the cool ground
in the middle of the field.
Prince lay down beside me, his fur
                              warming my side
as I watched the sky.

When you lie on your back in a bare field
and look straight up, all
you see is sky.

But when I tried to stand,
one leg was gone.
I only had one leg.

I WOKE, FELL BACK ASLEEP
and woke again. And I could see
my leg and foot wrapped in white
and propped on top of the covers.

But I didn't remember. Not yet.

Heard voices coming closer,
                              fading away.
"Her father let her...
          hanging on the back of that tractor...
imagine..."

When I opened my eyes,
my head was turned toward the window.
And all I could see out that window
was sky.

WHEN I WOKE UP ENOUGH
to look around, I knew
I was in hospital,
and it was a couple days later.

In that time my daddy tied Prince
up to the tractor shed
and shot him with his hunting rifle.

Daddy blamed Prince for the whole thing.
Not the hare.

MUM DIDN'T TELL ME RIGHT AWAY
about Prince and Dad.
But the nurses knew. I could tell
by the way they looked at me
they knew something I didn't.

I pestered Mum with questions.
When was Daddy coming to see me,
and couldn't Daddy bring Prince
so I could talk to him out the window?
                                    But Mum
just tightened her lips and changed the subject.
Until finally she told me the truth.

Every time I think about this,
the blood color from that room
in my head pours down
into my stomach
and I feel sick.

After he shot Prince, my daddy walked
off the farm and didn't come back.
He didn't take the car.
He didn't tell anybody
where he was going.

Now, whenever things are quiet —

                  as quiet as can be —

that rifle shot
goes off in my head,
just like that.

Boom.

DOCTOR CAME IN, SAW ME AWAKE,
said, "You gave your mum quite a scare,
young lady."
Nurse came in, said the same thing.
They never mentioned Dad.

Mum spent all her time with me.
There wasn't anybody at home
for her to take care of. We were everybody.
"Thank you, Reverend Douglas," Mum
                        would whisper to herself.

"Who's Reverend Douglas?" I asked.
And she said, "Tommy. Tommy Douglas,
the preacher who got elected
                        Premier of Saskatchewan
and got a law passed
so we don't have to pay to go to hospital."

"If it weren't for Reverend Douglas,
we'd surely be in the poorhouse," Mum said.

I didn't know what the poor house was,
or if there was one here in Souris.

But I learned soon enough
once Mum drove me home in the car
and rattled my wheelchair over the dirt

                                    and gravel
to the back door, and there was no Dad
banging in the shed,
and no Prince
running up to meet me.

I STAYED MORE THAN A WEEK IN HOSPITAL
before Dr. Phillips even mentioned
                              going home.
Then one morning he woke me up
early, flipped on all the lights
and said, "Congratulations!
You get to go home today."

The nurse took the tube
out of the back of my hand right then,
slapped on a bandaid and said
I should eat breakfast before I go.

By the time I started to put on some clothes
and get myself out of bed,
the pain medicine from that tube
had worn off. Whenever I started to move,
the bones in my leg tried to move, too.
                              The pain
shot up my leg and back down again.

Finally the nurse brought me
a blue pill and a glass of water.
"Just to get you home, honey," she said.

THAT HOT SPELL WE HAD DIDN'T LAST,
and the day I came home was wet,
half snowing, half raining.
Daddy loved that kind of weather in spring,
said it soaked right into the ground
and made the seeds sprout. Only thing was,
    Dad walked out
before we could get any seeds in the ground.

Mum made up the chesterfield as a bed for me.
I couldn't climb the stairs to my room,
and those first days I just lay real still
trying not to make the bones mad.

I had to work the wheelchair to get myself
over to the table for meals,
                    and the darned thing
would turn left and right on no notice. Couldn't
get that chair through the bathroom door, even.

LIVING ON THE CHESTERFIELD, I COULD LOOK OUT
the front window and see our big lilac bushes
swaying back and forth, hear the wind
whistling around the corner of our house.

That hot spell made the leaves spring open
and the lilacs burst out in purple flowers.

The way those lilacs would swing
in the wind like bells
made me think of a wedding going on.
The rain and snow getting married.

THE WHOLE TIME I WAS IN HOSPITAL
the only person who came
to see me was Miss Tollofsen,
my grade six teacher. At first
I thought I was in trouble
                    for missing school,
and Sadie the Dragon Lady
had come to my hospital room
to wave that long pointer she used
to slap at countries on the pull-down maps
or poke at the wrong answer
somebody'd written on the board.

But when she came to the hospital
she was different. She had the same
white hair, same long skirt, same
lace-up shoes that were so loud
when she walked down the hallways,
same pointy nose sticking way out of her face.

She brought a couple of my schoolbooks.
Said I didn't have to do
a whole page of math problems.
Just some.

Brought a card signed by the whole class.

Then she handed me some plain paper
                            and colored pencils.
Said maybe I'd like to draw pictures.

So I said thank you a bunch of times,
which I can't remember saying to her before,
because at school she seemed
                            cold as a mountain
with a lump of snow on top of her head
that never melted.

BLUE AS THE SKY, THAT CARD
signed by my class sat on the table
beside my bed. I'd pick it up and run my fingers
over the names. Jamie and Joey signed it
without writing anything insulting.
Mei Wang wrote in her curled handwriting
that reminded me of flowers,
                              "I am so sorry
you got hurt. May you come back soon."

Once Mei invited me over after school, said
we could pick oranges from the produce section
of her parents' store, the one
most folks call the Chink store.
Maybe she could teach me
to work the cash register, Mei said. I pleaded
        with Mum to let me go.
But Mum said no.

I took the colored pencils
and wore down the brown and black
                        drawing Prince,
while I still remembered
what he looked like. His black eyes,
straight-up ears. Brown streaks on his face.
So I'd never forget him.

Even after I got home from hospital
and started living on the chesterfield,
here came Miss Tollofsen
after she was done with school.

She got out of her car with a fist full
of lilac flowers, and I found out
we had something in common.

Mum put them in a glass of water
and I got to smell them. Dark purple ones
and light purple ones. Some still
                        tight little buds.
Even some white ones, and they all
smelled a little different.

She brought the whole spring day inside
when she did that.

ON LONELY DAYS WHEN NOBODY CAME,
and the Soo Line's wheels squealing
                        on the tracks
sounded like it was right outside our door,
when it was just us, Mum and me, in the house,
Mum sat in a chair and stared.

Didn't put on clean clothes. Just what she wore
the day before
and the day before that.
When the clock chimed twelve
she'd push herself up and fix us something to eat.
At five she did the same thing.
She took me to the bathroom.
But afterward, she sank back into that chair
like it wouldn't let go.

Out our front window
I could see the back end of the tractor
parked neatly in the machinery shed
like nothing had happened.

I couldn't see behind the shed
                        to the burn pile
where Prince's bones were lying,
and whenever Mum drove me in the car
to Dr. Phillips' office, I'd always
fix my eyes on something else.

DR. PHILLIPS WAS HANDSOME.
He didn't look like a farmer,
didn't have a funny tan
where a cap would've sat
across the middle of his forehead.
He never looked sweaty or greasy.
He took off my bandages
and the steel brace under the bandages
to check out how things
                    were coming along.

My leg looked like it was covered
with some crazy criss-crossed
train track — blue and black and green, puffy
with stitches all over the place
and the skin flaking off like snowflakes.
In the operating room, he put the bones
back straight. He stitched up stuff
under the skin, and then
he stitched up the top skin.

And every time we got home
from having Dr. Phillips turn my leg
back and forth just a bit, and from bumping it
getting in and out of the car, I'd sink back
into the chesterfield and close my eyes.
I'd lie there until the pain
decided to slide out of my leg
and quietly sneak away.

WHENEVER SOMEBODY DROVE INTO THE YARD,
or I heard what sounded like footsteps
coming up to the door, I'd jump, hoping
                              it was Dad.

He couldn't stand
to be away from us, not knowing
how I was. He wanted to apologize
for what he'd done to Prince,
and he knew he'd better get back
                              to farming.

Even if it was just the house creaking
or Harry Record driving his pickup
too fast down the dirt road past our house,
something in me tried to turn it
into a Dad sound.

Then everything would settle down again
to where I could hear a big semi on the highway
a long ways off, or a train banging
                              its cars together
down by the elevators.

One of the times I thought Dad
had come home, it was really
Joey and Jamie's dad, Harry Record.
I heard stomping up the front steps.
The doorbell rang. And I knew
                              it wasn't Dad.

Well, Harry Record
took off his cap,
and his hair was flattened
to his head. He said Vida told him
Mum wanted to talk to him,
and I wondered why
she was calling over a man she never liked
just to talk. So I lay on the chesterfield
real quiet, and listened.

Mum was looking for someone to seed our fields.

She sat him down at the kitchen table
and started drawing up a contract
like she'd done that sort of thing
all her life.

They drank coffee
and talked about hard spring wheat
and how much moisture we got
in that wet stretch. How far down
till you hit dry dirt again.

And Harry said, "You don't want to plant
wheat. Can't sell it. All our bins
is full of the stuff. Last year, Wheat Board
bought four bushels to the acre. Four.
Some folks got wheat two years old
piled up on the ground.
Wheat ain't worth nothing."

And Mum said, "What are you planting
this year, Harry?" Knowing it'd be wheat,
and Harry just grunted into his coffee.

Harry said, "Some farmers is starting
to seed flax, some mustard. Don't
know how it'll go. Always
gone with wheat. This here's
wheat-growing country."

"Fine," said Mum. "We'll seed everything
to flax. A bit of mustard."

Harry didn't want the work
of seeding our fields with strange

new crops.
"You want to plant that fancy
experimental stuff, you go right ahead.
Just get you a gorilla from over at the Mental.
He won't care what you tell him to plant."

And Harry got up from the table
and walked straight out the door
without signing any piece of paper.

MISS TOLLOFSEN CAME OVER WEARING PANTS.
"It's such a lovely day," she said.
"Thought I'd walk."

Mum pulled a chair up
so Miss Tollofsen could sit down.
Handed her a cup of coffee.

It was Saturday, same day
Harry Record came over.
I didn't want to talk schoolwork
                    on a Saturday.
It's a personal rule I have.
But then she asked if I'd done any pictures
with the paper and colored pencils
she gave me. I reached under the chesterfield
where I kept my books and papers
and my drawings of Prince.

She looked at each one real close.
"My, what a handsome dog.
Is this the dog — "

I nodded, and Dad and Prince
started to march right out of that room in my head.

When Miss Tollofsen stood up to leave
in her navy blue pants, Mum followed
and they talked in low voices
out on the porch.

Took me all afternoon
to get that door inside my head
shut again.

MUM WORE LIPSTICK
the day
we saw Dr. Phillips again.
He took out the stitches on my leg,
took off the metal brace.
Covered my leg in a hard white cast.
                    Heavy, too.
Gave me a set of crutches and a pat on the back.

No more wheelchair.
And I could sleep in my own bed.

MUM DIDN'T SAY MUCH
about my new cast or crutches.
I thought she'd be happy.
But that evening over supper, I knew
she was thinking hard
        about something else.
A piece of hair kept falling out
from behind her ear.
                Mum's hair
went a whole lot grayer up at the top of her head
in the time after Dad left. And that one piece
she'd put back and put back behind her ear.

When she does that it means she's thinking.
She's working something out.

What I didn't know
was that Angus was coming.

ONE MORNING EARLY
while I was still in bed,
I heard the crunch of feet on gravel, then stomp
                        up the porch steps.
I sat up, listening.

Doorbell. Not Dad.

I slumped back onto my pillow,
the sun slanting
across the end of my bed.

Mum's voice.
Two men's voices.
Mum went outside.

I heard the tractor start up. Heard its gears
grind as it backed up. It came
around the house, growling
and grinding, into the field.
I pulled myself out of bed
and peered out my window.

Soon as they saw me sticking my head out,
Jamie and Joey ran up.

"Hey, Em! You know
there's a gorilla in your field?"

I squinted.
The man driving the tractor was huge.
He was pale white, like he hadn't been outdoors
in years. And he had orange hair.

"That's no gorilla," I said.
                    "He's got orange hair."
"He's an orange-a-tan!" they yelled,
and they hunched their backs
and swung their arms,
making low animal noises.

I hopped out the door of my room
and waited at the top of the stairs
till the other man left
                    and Mum came back in.

"Who's in the field?" I asked.
She tilted her head back, her lips
flat and serious. "That man
          is from the Mental.
Stay away from him."

Last Halloween, Joey
dressed up as a mental patient.
He wrapped himself in toilet paper
from head to foot, rubbed charcoal
around his eyes and stuck on
a rubber nose, crooked and warty.

I got dressed, put a shoe on my good foot,
hopped down the stairs with my crutches
in one hand and my other hand
                              on the stair rail.

Then I was through the kitchen
                    and out the back door.
Mrs. Record stood on her porch
with a dish towel in her hands,
calling her boys in.

People from town
started driving by. "Hey, Hopalong!
Heard you got a sub-human out here,"
Frank the mechanic called to me.
"Better stay inside. Lock your doors.
See, I got my car doors locked."

I didn't know how
the man on the tractor
was real quick gonna jump off
a moving tractor and attack
Frank sitting in his car.
The man was way out in the field.

"You get yourself inside, Hopalong."

I didn't like being called Hopalong.
And if the man on the tractor
                    could hear the names
people were calling him,
I'd a bet he wouldn't like it either.

I WAS DRAGGING AROUND A LOT OF MAD
when I opened the door
and made my way
into the kitchen.

Mum sat at the table
talking on the phone. The lines
on her face stood out. "I was assured
by the hospital personnel that this man
is not a threat to society."
I could hear a teeny tiny voice
inside the phone yelling, "You're crazy
to let an insane person
around your own home!"

Mum didn't say goodbye.
She just hung up. Loudly.
Neither of us was in a good mood
when I said, "I want to know why
Dad isn't seeding the field.
I want to know where Dad is
and when he's coming back."

Mum stood up, her chair scraping the floor.
"What I know is he's not here.

He left me
with a critically injured child, no money,
no crop, and bins full of wheat
not worth a hill of beans.
What am I supposed to do?
Sit by and let us starve?"

I looked at Mum.
She seemed old and bony, that gray
growing out of her head
where there used to be dark,

chestnut-colored hair.
Her fingers wrinkled
where she gripped the chair.
And her eyes had dark circles under them.

I was mad at Mum for looking old.
I was mad at Dad for walking away.
And I was mad at myself

for the way it all started.

"It's my fault Daddy left."
And I started backing out of the kitchen.

Mum's voice got real quiet.
"No. It was not your fault, Emmie.
It was just the last straw…"

Then the doorbell rang. Harry Record.
Mum answered. Harry was pulling off his cap.
          "Now, Clarice, we don't want
             to get murdered in our own beds,"
    he was saying, a little laugh in his voice.
"Of course I'd a worked your fields. I didn't really
think you'd go and do it..."

Mum tightened her mouth flat.
I slipped through the kitchen and out the door,
thumped down the back steps,
the shoelace flapping
on my one good foot.

I FOUND A RUSTED CHAIR, DUSTED
out the seat, and sat down
to watch the crazy man
seed our fields.

Felt something beside me. *Prince,*
I thought, and reached out my hand
                        to pet him.
Then I realized
one of my crutches
had fallen against my lap.

I sat in that chair
and cried
while the man on our tractor,
his shocking orange hair
shining in the sun,
sowed round
after round
of seeds
into the dirt.

WITH TEARS IN YOUR EYES
everything looks different.
Like a watercolor painting.
The trees look prettier. All that winterkill,
the dead branches that spring storms
nipped in the bud,
smear together with the green.

I was deep in my own brain
sitting in that rusted chair
when Mum called out the kitchen window,
"Em! Come get your dinner!"
And I came out of myself
to notice it was quiet.
The tractor was still. And the tractor man
was sitting on the back step
eating off one of our plates.

I couldn't decide if I should go to the trouble
to hobble all the way around
to the front porch to avoid him,
or if I should try to just slide past him
there on the back step.
Mum called again, looking down
out of the window over the sink.
So I started toward the back step. I got closer
                         to the crazy man.
My hands gripped hard
on the handles of my crutches.

My good foot landed in front of the step
where he sat eating off our blue plate
with the chip on one side.
All of a sudden he put his plate down
on the ground, and he bent over
and tied up my shoelace.

Then he picked the plate up again.
Before I got all the way to the door
he said, "Tell your mama Angus says
she cooks real good."

"Angus says you cook real good,"
I repeated to Mum in the kitchen.
"Who?" she asked,
her eyebrows wrinkled.
"Angus," I said,
pointing my thumb out the door.

I ate up a pile of Mum's macaroni and cheese
with ham, and a slice of Jell-O salad.
Then I went to my room to think.
My leg swung into that rectangle
                              of sunlight
on the floor. I flopped down on my bed
and lifted up the mattress
to count the days since Dad left.

Maybe I'll count, too, each day
Angus is here,
        or I'll start a list —
Things to Know about Angus the Crazy Man:
One. He's got a name.
Two. He's not a gorilla.

Far as I know,
there's never been a gorilla
that can tie a shoelace.

Angus

EVERY MORNING,
Angus from the mental hospital
starts up our tractor with the seeder attached
and drives around the side of the house
                              and out to the fields.

Every noon he shuts the tractor down
in whatever place it's in. He starts walking
from way out in the field, and then he waits
                              on the back step
for Mum to bring him a plate of food.
Same blue plate. Same chip on the side.
                              Glass of water.
It's quiet while Angus eats.

When the tractor's shut down, I can hear
meadowlarks calling from the fence posts.
One calling, another answering.

Then I look out my window
and I see there's a meadowlark perched
on the drainpipe at the very corner
of the roof of our house.
And there's Angus
sitting on the back steps,
whistling sure as can be,
just like a meadowlark.

And that meadowlark on the drainpipe
is singing back.

NIGHTS I LIE AWAKE A LONG TIME
listening to all the sounds. Wind. Trains.
Angus coming in from seeding.
Watch the sky fade to darkness. Nine,
ten o'clock. Watch light from the moon
inch across my floor.

I think about Dad. How
in the world could someone
                    just disappear?
Like snow on a windy day.

How far can a person get to, walking?
I'm thinking he's got to be nearby
somewhere. Maybe in town.

Then I think about the words
Mum used. Last straw.
Soon I mean to ask her
about the other straws.

THAT TRACTOR LOOKS LIKE A LITTLE RED TOY
out there in the fields.
When Angus finishes his dinner
he gets smaller and smaller,
walking back across the fields
till he gets to be smaller than the tractor.
Then he climbs on.

I hear that tractor rumbling
all afternoon. Day after day.
At five o'clock, Angus stops the tractor again.
Comes to the porch step for supper.

Angus waits on the step
for Mum or me to hand him
his plate of food.
Same plate. Same chip on the side.
Mum keeps it separate.

Then he goes out till it's so dark
you can't see anything, and I hear
the empty seeder rattling
            around the side of the house,
going to park in the shed.
Tractor shuts down.

Angus sleeps in the machinery shed
under a blanket. He's stuck himself
behind the discer, sprayer,
the two-ton truck with the dead battery.
                              Won't go back
to the mental hospital to sleep.
If it was me, I wouldn't go either,
no matter where
I had to sleep.

MUM PARKED THE CAR IN TOWN
 by Dr. Phillips' office this morning,
just up the block from the King Koin laundromat.
I got out of the car and onto my crutches.

                       Then I turned around
and thought I saw Dad
walking out of King Koin
           and rounding the corner.

I didn't get a good look at him,
but from out of the side of my eye
the man was the size and shape of Dad.
I straightened up and looked real hard,
but the man was gone.

I didn't tell Mum, just kept it
inside myself. But all the way home
                it swirled in my head
like laundry in one of those machines,
that man coming out of King Koin.

I'm starting to wonder just what makes a person
                                 crazy.

MUM AND DR. PHILLIPS DECIDED
I could go back to school.
They didn't ask me. Besides,
there were only two weeks left.

Monday morning Mum got me up.
I put on a skirt and blouse,
and Mum dug my schoolbooks out
from under the chesterfield,
and she drove me to school.

Mum walked in with me,
carried my books. Mei Wang
grinned when she saw me, said
to Mum, "I can carry her books,"
and she did.

Mum and Miss Tollofsen
stood outside the classroom talking
while most of the class followed me
to my desk beside Mei's,
and they asked me questions.
"Did your foot get cut all the way off?
Joey said he saw it and it was all the way off."

"Have you seen that crazy man up close?"
"Is he cross-eyed?"
                    "Does he drool?"

"My dad says never let a crazy person
get hold of a pair of scissors, 'cause once
a mental patient was cutting paper
with some scissors, and he turned around
and cut this guy's ear right off."

Everybody wanted to sign my cast,
but then Miss Tollofsen came in
and clapped her hands and everyone
dove into their seats.

I stayed all the way through recess
until lunch time. But I felt hot
and my leg ached. I put my head
down on my desk. Mei walked up
to Miss Tollofsen. Then
Miss Tollofsen came over
and felt my forehead.

"Honey, you look peaked. I believe
you've had enough school
for one day." And she called
Mum to pick me up.

EVERY NIGHT, MUM LOCKS THE DOORS.
Never did before. That is,
before Angus came.

What I figure is, if he
was going to do something to us
like cut our ears off, he
would've done it by now.
He could just sneak into the house
during the day and grab the scissors
while Mum's turned her back or something.

If he wanted to. But I think
he likes her cooking too much.
And I checked.
He doesn't look cross-eyed to me.

Things to Know
about Angus the crazy man:
Three. He can speak Meadowlark.
Four. He sees colors all around people.

This is how I found out about number four.
After supper I went outside to sit
on the front steps, and I saw
Angus didn't go straight out to the tractor
after he finished eating on the back porch. He went
into the shed. Stayed there awhile.

I acted like I was going across the yard
and then I turned toward the shed
and tried to peer through cracks
in the boards.

He'd saved his piece of bread from supper
and was feeding it to some mice.

He'd hold the bread real still
and after a bit here came
a couple little brown mice
no bigger than his thumb,
and they ate the bread
right out of his fingers.

I was trying to find the best crack
to look through when Angus said,
"If you come up real quiet and slow,
maybe you can feed 'em."

I felt like taking off at a run,
but I couldn't. And I was afraid Mum
might see me going in the shed
and come haul me inside.

But I inched up as quiet as I could
on creaky crutches to where Angus was.
I turned over a bucket and sat on it.

Angus was red as a beet from the neck up,
                           from the arms down.
I took the piece of bread he held out for me.

I had to wait holding the bread.
The mice scattered when I came so close.
But after a bit they scooted back. They ate
from Angus's fingers. Then
they ate from mine.

One even grabbed my finger
with its little paws while it took the bread
and scampered off.
                I didn't say anything.
Finally Angus said, "They got such pretty colors
around 'em. Blue and orange and yellow."

"Really?" I said, squinting, trying to see colors
surrounding their little fur coats.
"Yep," says Angus.
                "Everybody got colors.
Animals and people."

"Angus likes your colors," says Angus.

I'm wondering what colors I've got
around me. Angus says blue like lilacs,
pinky colors and some green.

I'm wondering if seeing colors around people
means you're crazy.

PEOPLE DON'T DRIVE BY OUR PLACE
to take a look at the crazy man anymore.
First couple days Angus was seeding,
people drove past like they were looking
                              at Christmas lights.

But after a few days peeking out their car windows
and seeing a man out in a field
                              on a tractor,
they got bored. Went home.

JOEY AND JAMIE CAME UP TO ME
before school and said,
"Everybody knows
your dad's living down at the El Rancho.
Working for the railroad.
Our dad's talked to him tons of times."

Mei was holding my books.
I just stood there. Then I realized
my mouth was hanging open.

"So have I," I lied, and Mei and I
pushed right between them.

Small town,
seems like everybody knows your business
before you do.

TOOK HIM TWO WEEKS, BUT ANGUS
finished seeding this afternoon.
He backed the seeder into the shed,
took it off the tractor. Parked the tractor.
Then he came around the back door
                              and knocked.
Talked with Mum.

Next thing I knew Angus was taking a shovel
and carrying it back of the shed.
He was there a long time.

I broke my vow never to go back there.
I peeked around the corner of the shed
and there he was, digging a big hole.

So I moved closer, and Angus said,
"Those bones been calling to Angus
every night. Been crying out.
Gotta put those bones to rest."

Mum was hanging sheets on the clothesline.
She knew I was there with Angus,
but she let me be. I spent the rest of the day
helping him bury Prince.
Bones black as soot.

Wind blew dirt into our faces, moaned
when it bent around the corner of our house,
flapped the sheets on the line.

NOW FARMERS ARE WATCHING THE SKY.
Soon as seeds are in the ground
is the best time for rain, they say.

They're saying, no rain
and those seeds'll just bake
in an oven of dirt.

I'm looking at the sky, too.
Got to have clouds first
if you want rain.

DR. PHILLIPS SAWED OFF MY OLD CAST.
Put on a new one,
a walking cast.
Got a rubber pad under my foot where
I'm supposed to start putting weight on it.

One thing he didn't discuss with us until today
is the fact that my hurt leg
is going to be shorter than the other.
Mum asked, "Won't it grow out?"
And Dr. Phillips looked at her
                    like he was a teacher
explaining a new word to the class.
"No, it won't grow out."

Said it might not even grow
when the other leg does.
"We'll have to watch it," he said.

Mum says when a doctor tells you he's
going to watch it, it means
he'll look at it in about a year
                    and then tell you
what you can already see for yourself.

IT'S HOT.
Wind's blowing dirt across the fields.
Not enough moisture to keep the dirt down.

We have to close our windows, and with Mum
baking bread, it's hot in the house.

I kneaded the dough. Sprinkled a bit of flour
on the table. Slammed the dough down.
Shoved my hands into it, turned it over,
did the same thing. Hard work,
but I feel good when it's done.

While I was kneading, I screwed up my courage
to ask Mum about Dad. What made him leave.
"Oh, I don't want to talk about that,"
                    Mum said real quick,
like I was asking her to tell me about a bad dream.

She was hoping I'd shut up about it.
But I didn't.

I could feel her staring hard at my back.
I slammed the dough onto the table
                    and punched at it.
Then Mum slumped down into a kitchen chair
like she was a pile of tired laundry.
But she told me.

"Your father never wanted to be a farmer."
I turned my head and my eyes
bored right into her face.

"Wanted to be a train engineer.
But as the only boy in the family, his father
said he had to take on the farm.
Sisters got married. Moved to Medicine Hat,
Swift Current. Nobody but Dad
to carry on with farming.

There were years of drought
when wind blew everything away.
Once, he tried grazing cattle
but lost three-quarters of the herd
                              in winter blizzards.
Hailstorms came
                 and flattened most of what grew.
What he managed to harvest
he couldn't sell. Wheat Board
                              wouldn't buy it.
Wheat lay in heaps on the ground,
bins already full.

Three years ago it rained.
There was so much rain, nothing grew
                                    but dockweed.
Couldn't get into a field with a tractor.
Most fields were under water till the middle of July.

It was enough to make a man want to give up,
walk away from farming. But he stayed.
        Until your accident," Mum told me.

I glanced down at my scarred and shortened leg,
my new cast already gathering dirt.

"He blamed himself," Mum said.

"No, he blamed Prince," I shot back.

"He blamed himself," she said again.
"He took it out on Prince."

AFTER ANGUS GOT DONE SEEDING,
Mum thought there wasn't much reason
for him to stay.

But I wanted him to,
so I've been trying to think
of things Angus could do
        to be useful around here.
Like work on the garden, fix the gate.

But today, problem's solved.
Car broke down.
The garage man wants two hundred dollars
          to fix it.
Mum says we don't have two hundred dollars.
Don't even have enough to buy
a new battery for the two-ton.

Only car that works now is the tractor.
And Angus is the only one
        who knows how to drive it.

ANGUS SAYS
you never know what you'll find
if you poke around farm buildings.

While I was at school
he rummaged through the shed
and found an old tractor seat. He
figured out a way to attach it
to our tractor beside the first seat.
By the time I got home,
he'd taken an old wicker
                          laundry basket
that had been collecting dust
and wired the basket on behind both seats.

Mum looked it over.
"Guess it's better than going hungry,"
she said, and handed us a grocery list.

Me and Angus drove over to OK Economy.
Slowed down traffic. Parked in the lot.
Angus helped me down
and we went in.

At first
there seemed to be lots of customers in the store.
Then the aisles started clearing of people
until we were practically the only ones shopping.

Angus just followed me around,
got things off the top shelves.
Pretty soon here came Mr. McGillvary,
store manager. Patted my head, asked
how I'm doing.

"Fine, thanks."
That's when I realized
all the customers were at the front of the store.
Not even a cash register ringing.

Mr. McGillvary didn't look at Angus
directly, just out of the corner of his eye.

When we walked up to the cash registers,
the check-out ladies backed away.
Mr. McGillvary had to check us out himself.

Probably a dozen people watched us leave.
Angus says they had a lot of red around them.
Red's not good, says Angus.

MIDDLE OF LAST NIGHT SOMETIME
it started to rain.
Rained all day today.

I'm thinking maybe Daddy
gave up farming
                one year too soon.

TODAY IN THE PAPER
I saw three letters people had written, complaining
about patients from the mental hospital
running loose around town.

All three letter writers — Ed Spiske,
Opal Evans and Irene Inglesham —
were in the store when me and Angus walked in,
                                    did our shopping.
Irene's a cashier in that store.

Letters said mental cases shouldn't be allowed
going into our shops and walking our streets.
Not without the company of a hospital staff person
who can wrestle them to the ground
                                    if need be,
force them into straitjackets.
Asked the chief constabulary officer,
                        D'Arcy Pettit,
to keep the deranged from creating chaos
and disorder in our peaceful town.

All we did
was shop for groceries.
On a tractor.

AFTER THAT RAIN
we got some strong sun.
Heated the ground like a greenhouse.
Now little green mounds are starting
to spread over the dark soil.

WHEN WE DROVE THE TRACTOR
to OK Economy, Angus
pointed to the buildings and the gardens
at the mental hospital.

"That's my garden," he said.
"That's where my room was —
                              second floor,
third window from the right.
First floor's where we ate.
Mrs. Reiss was my favorite nurse.
Always treated me nice. Never
tied me down."

I think that's what he said.
But I'm not sure. Tractor was loud.

A MAN FROM THE MENTAL HOSPITAL
came by today to check on Angus,
see how he was doing. Mum
and Angus and the man walked
                          around the fields,
looked at the garden. I sat
on the porch steps and listened
best I could. The man said Angus
was the best gardener they ever had.

Mum looked at the man. Then
she looked at Angus. "Oh," she said,
like she'd never thought about
Angus knowing how to do anything
except be crazy.

JOEY RECORD SAYS
my dad's heading out on a freight train.
Going to get rich working that train
over the mountains to Vancouver.
Joey thinks he knows everything.
                                    Most things
he makes up in his own head.
I told Joey my dad
would never leave town without
                            telling me first.
What I figure is, if I can get Dad
to come see the green in our fields,
he'll be back to farming.

MISS TOLLOFSEN CALLED.
Invited me to her house for tea.
Mum made me wear a dress.

She picked me up in her big bug car.
I was waiting for her at the window,
started down our front steps
before she'd closed her car door.

Angus was clanking around
in the machinery shed. And Miss Tollofsen
strode straight and tall over to Angus
and stuck out her hand. Introduced herself.

She knew all about him. Everybody in town
knows there's a crazy man on the loose,
and some insane people are letting him
                                   work for them.

In her class, she always said
                 every day is a fresh start.
No matter what hijinks
someone had done the day before, or
what condition you came to school in yesterday,
it stayed in that day. Didn't spill over.

I like that.

WE DROVE UP MISS TOLLOFSEN'S DRIVEWAY,
two strips of cement, middle strip of grass.
Her house is old and warm
and smells like someone's been living there,
cooking there, putting on perfume there
for a long time. So many good smells.

We made sugar cookies together.
When they were cooling,
we went out to her backyard,
sat in chairs with cushions around a little table.

Miss Tollofsen introduced me
                to all her rose bushes.
I smelled each one. I said, "My mum
always said roses can't grow here."

Miss Tollofsen smiled.
"It's not impossible, just difficult. Now,
your mother may be quite right
about growing roses where you are.
Too much wind. In town it's easier.
You see? I put up this wood fence
                precisely to grow roses.
You have to protect them a little, and then
cut them back hard. It sounds harsh,
but adversity makes them thrive.
Then they'll reward you
                by blooming their hearts out."

She cut some velvety yellow ones
and we set them in a vase on our table.
                              Then we had tea.
I paid close attention to my manners,
napkin in my lap, and leaned over my plate
so I wouldn't crumb everything up.

In the time I was having tea with Miss Tollofsen,
three people came by, all her former students.
Miss Tollofsen introduced me and said,
                    "Emaline is an artist."

I'd never thought of myself as an artist.
But she said it the same way
        she once said to our class,
                        "Glenn Gould is a pianist."

Later I rode home in her car, tin of cookies
on my lap, roses wrapped in a wet dish towel.
She suggested I enter some of my art work
in the fair coming up the beginning of July.

Lately I've thought of myself
as a girl with big pieces missing — Dad, Prince,
part of a leg.

When I had tea with Miss Tollofsen
I felt whole again.

OUR FLAX HAS STARTED TO BLOOM.
So has the mustard.
Mustard's bright yellow. Flax is light blue.

Day by day the blossoms take over
the green color of the plants.
Day by day I look out and see
                    more yellow, more blue.
I try to find pencil crayons in the right colors
to draw the picture filling my window.

Me and Angus walked out into the fields,
felt the flowers, smelled them. Rolled dirt
between our fingers.

I asked him what these fields
smelled like to him.
"Angus smells happiness," he said.

ANGUS WALKED TO TOWN
by himself today to get a tractor part.
Walked into the farm implement dealership.
Asked for the part.
Bought it.

D'Arcy Pettit picked Angus up
halfway home. Said Don Ojala
was sure Angus had stolen something
out of his store.

Angus turned all his pockets
inside out. Took off his shoes.
Took off his socks. Constable Pettit
made him lean against the police cruiser
while he ran his hands
up and down Angus, searching
for whatever Don Ojala thought he'd stole.

Then he dropped Angus off
in our front yard. Told Mum
he'd had to look into it since Don
called with a complaint. Asked Mum
        if she'd had any trouble with Angus.
Mum shook her head. "None," she said.
"He's been a good worker."
It was more than I expected her to say.

Half hour later I found Angus
sitting on his blankets in the shed,

                               shaking.

I told him
next time he goes to town,
let me go with him.
Some people can be dangerous
when they're afraid.

WE HAD A PARTY AT SCHOOL TODAY.
End of the year. Me and Mum
brought cupcakes.

At the end of the party, Miss Tollofsen
handed out our report cards.

I had a whole bunch of butterflies
bumping in my stomach
when I opened mine,
even though Miss Tollofsen smiled
when I took it from her.

All A's and B's.
I wanted to show Mum first thing.
Maybe Angus, too.

Wish Dad
could see my report card.
But Dad was never much interested
                                in school.

LAST NIGHT I DREAMED
about Dad, about Prince.
Dad was looking for Prince,
holding his shotgun.

I hid Prince under my bed.
I could hear Dad's footsteps on the stairs,
Mum calling him to come back down
while I stood by my bed guarding Prince
underneath, shaking. I waited
for Dad to open the door.

I woke up. Had to turn on the light,
check the stairs, look
                    under my bed.
Lay back in bed with the light still on
and listened to my heart pound in my chest.

I wonder why
I want so much to find Dad
when he shot my best friend.

But he's still my dad.
And I want him to come home.

FILLED OUT THE ENTRY FORM FOR THE FAIR.
Taped my 25 cents to the form and sent it in.

I looked over all my drawings of Prince
and made a group of three. Then
I entered them in the Junior Art section
under "Hand Drawing: Animals."
                        Addressed the envelope.
Dropped it in the post box.

You have to take the pictures in
just before the fair starts.
I'm going to try to walk over there
with my pictures, figure it's about halfway
to the El Rancho.

And I want to get to the El Rancho.

Dad

I'VE GONE TO THE JULY 1ST PARADE
as long as I can remember, so I
begged Mum to take me, promised
I could walk the ten blocks to Main Street.
Actually, I wanted to see if I could do it, see
how I felt when I got through
walking that whole way.

Mum said yes.

Parade started out with Constable Pettit
dressed in his Mounted Policeman's uniform —
red jacket, dark pants, broad hat, boots —
and he rode his horse, Titan, holding the reins
in one hand and a big new flag
                              in the other.

I like the new flag. Some don't,
don't like anything new or different.

Mei and her sisters tossed candies
from the back of their Wang's Grocery truck.

Watching the parade made me think
     about a picture I saw in the Weekly Reader
newspaper we get at school,
about a parade in Selma, Alabama,
where a preacher named Dr. King
and some others marched across a bridge.
The picture showed police on horseback
               and on foot with clubs,
waiting for the marchers to cross the bridge.
Couple little girls in that picture
wore patent leather shoes and coats
like they were on their way to church,
and they were each holding somebody's hand,
marching right toward those policemen.

People here say Dr. King's a communist,
gets paid by the Russians to stir up trouble.
And now at this parade I wanted so bad
to go to, it's that march in Selma
I'm thinking about.

WALK HOME WAS HARD. I WAS TIRED.
But I made it on my own two feet.

When me and Mum rounded the corner
of the mental hospital, I saw two cars
parked in front of our house.
Mum hurried ahead and I came up behind.
                              Mr. McGillvary
and another man from OK Economy
were talking to Angus.

Angus stood in the middle of Mum's garden,
                          weeds in his hands.
Looked like he was having a nightmare,
shaking his head, yelling.

Mr. McGillvary and the other man
said someone stole a coffee can full of cash
from a back room of the store.
One of the stock boys mentioned
Angus's name.

Already they'd plowed through
the tractor shed, lifted up his blankets,
torn into his little suitcase of clothes.
Found nothing.

ABOUT AN HOUR LATER, CONSTABLE PETTIT
drove up, still dressed in his fancy uniform.
Said until this thing gets worked out,
he's got to arrest Angus.

Mum didn't even argue. Just stood there.
But I said Angus had done nothing wrong.
"We vouch for his good character," I told him.
It was something I heard
the man from the mental hospital

say about Angus.

"Well, you and your mum may just need to do that
in court, little miss," Constable Pettit said
as he loaded Angus into the back

of his police car.

I stood on the front step
long after that car turned
out of sight. I watched until the dust
from our driveway and the dirt road
settled out of the air. Then I sat

on our front steps
feeling like somebody'd reached inside me
and pulled my insides straight out.

MUM AND I ATE IN SILENCE.
Just the sound of forks scraping.
Angus's plate and glass
clean and quiet
beside the sink.

WENT TO THE FAIR,
even though I didn't feel like going anywhere.

Found the Coliseum where the art show
was taking place on the cement floor
                                      of the hockey rink.
Didn't know where my pictures
had been hung, so I just started by the front door,
examining all the drawings and paintings.

Some had ribbons on them. I never thought
about whether there'd be ribbons.
I was so caught up in seeing how someone else
had painted this grain elevator or that field,
I hardly noticed when I got around the room
to the junior section and my group of three
                                    pictures of Prince.

And my hand flew right up to my mouth.
Attached to the corner was the biggest
ribbon I ever saw — purply red with gold print —
                                    "Best Junior Exhibit."

DIDN'T WANT TO TELL MUM
right away about winning
a ribbon at the fair.
I wanted to hold it in me for awhile.

I walked out the big front gate under the sign
SOUTH SASKATCHEWAN AGRICULTURAL EXHIBITION
while crowds of people poured in,
and I stopped and felt the sun
and wind on my skin. Then I did it.

I walked the rest of the way to the El Rancho.

I opened the front door. It was cool
                              and dark inside.

I had to wait for my eyes to adjust
and while I was standing there
a lady said, "Can I help you?"

She stood behind the front desk
and her name tag said LOUISE.

I looked around and asked, "Which room
is Cal Bitterman's?"
And Louise said, "That's 209.
But you won't find him there. He's left for work.
You his daughter?"

I nodded.
She laughed. "Know how I could tell?
That cast on your leg. Cal told me
                    about the accident.
I always say if it don't kill you,
it'll make you strong."

I didn't know whether to go or stay.
Finally Louise said, "You want to leave a note?
I'll get you some paper."

I took the pen that was hanging on a chain
and wrote,
Dad,
My leg is lots better. Please
come home.
                    Emmie
P.S. You should see our fields.

I folded the paper and wrote *Cal Bitterman*.
I slid it across the big wooden counter.
Thanked her.

"I'll see he gets it," Louise said.

It was hard walking back home.
I told Mum about my ribbon,
but didn't tell
where I'd gone after that.

I GOT MUM TO HELP ME
make Angus a cake
with the rhubarb he'd been tending
                    in Mum's garden.
It was big and red and full, and when
we were standing there with garden plants
around our knees, I said, "It looks nice.
Not a weed anywhere."
Mum shook her head. "I just don't know
what we'd have done without him."

We took the rhubarb into the house,
scrubbed the dirt off in the sink,
pulled off the strings. Chopped it up.
Put it in a pot of water on the stove,
added a whole cup of sugar and cooked it.

Then I cut up some bread and toasted the cubes
in the oven. I dumped the toast cubes
                    into a casserole dish,
and then Mum poured in some eggs and cinnamon
and more sugar she'd mixed together.
We poured some hot milk
and melted butter over that
and baked it.

Mum says it's really a pudding, but it looks
                    like a cake to me.

We walked down to the police station,
met Constable Pettit with the warm cake
wrapped in one of Mum's tea towels.
He made us cut it up in front of him,
put a section on a plate to give to Angus.

Angus was the only prisoner in the jail.
I took him his slice of cake.

He was hunched over, looking at the floor.
"Angus didn't steal a thing,"
was all he said.

TOOK A SLICE OF BREAD OUT TO THE SHED.
Fed Angus's mice.
Picked up his blankets and the clothes
in his little suitcase, and my hand
hit something hard.

I pushed the clothes aside.
In a corner of that beat-up old suitcase
was a piece of model train. Little caboose
with SOO LINE painted across the side.

Me and Mum washed everything,
dried it on the line, folded his laundry.
Put it all back.

Now I can't get it out of my head,
that big man carrying around
a little boy's toy.

ANGUS STAYED IN JAIL FIVE DAYS
before somebody found the coffee can
of cash they were looking for.

A stock boy at OK Economy took the cash.
His name was Angus, too.
His mum found it under his bed,
half the money already spent.

When the other stock boy said, "Angus
took the money," Mr. McGillvary
jumped to the wrong person.

Mum's ears went red when she heard.
"Might've looked under their noses first," she said.

We're shopping at Wang's
from now on. Mum
even said so.

WE DIDN'T USED TO HAVE TV,
just listened to radio. Out here,
we can't get more than one
TV channel anyway.

Then about a year ago, Mum
walked into McTavish's Drug,
                    and it just so happened
that she was their something-thousandth customer.
The prize was a brand new color TV.
Mum even got her picture in the paper
for winning that TV.

Sometimes I watch our one channel,
but just about all that's on is news — war
                              in Vietnam,
America trying to stamp out communism.

I saw the news about our prime minister
making a speech down in Philadelphia
and saying the U.S. should try to talk to Hanoi,
                              work something out.
Canadians figured
since he'd won the Nobel Peace Prize,
our Mr. Pearson would be respected.

President Johnson grabbed him by the collar,
shook him, screamed in his face.

Guess not.

LOTS OF PEOPLE
are interested in our crops.
We've had farmers drive by
from up near Melfort, Ituna,
over from Moose Jaw.
They see our mustard and flax blooming
                                    yellow and blue
all the way to the edges of our land,
and they stop in, want to learn all about it.
Those fields just like a new car.
People want to kick the tires,
peek under the hood.

And they don't have a clue
                        about Angus —
talk to him an hour or more, wade
into the fields, figure Angus
is the expert, after all. Start back
to their cars, talk some more
with the car door open, Mum watching
from inside the house. Then
they smile, thank him, shake his hand.
Go on their way.

I TOLD MUM IT WAS TIME
to let Angus eat at the table with us.
It didn't feel right
us sitting around the kitchen table
with an empty chair, and him
sitting on the back step,
eating the same food
with dirt blown into it.

Mum stood over the stove
frying ham and hashbrowns,
the two skillets popping and snapping.
Finally she nodded her head.

Angus wouldn't come in at first.
I had to have Mum call out the door,
"Angus, dinner's on the table. Now
you come in and sit." And he did.
Mum has a way of saying things
so you just don't argue.

That big moose of a man walked in,
                              his boots clunking
across the kitchen floor.
When he sat in Dad's chair,
he made the table look small.

I PUT GLASSES OF MILK ON THE TABLE
for all of us. Mum passed the food around.
We ate in silence except for Mum
clearing her throat about five times
till she said, "Angus, don't you
have family around somewhere?"

Angus didn't look up. Looked at his plate.
"If there is, Angus don't know about it."

After a bit, Mum tried again. "No brothers
or sisters? Cousins? Parents passed on?"

"Don't know," says Angus, shoveling fried potatoes
into his mouth. "Angus grew up in a foster home,
then hospital since the age of seventeen."

Silence again. I looked at Mum, then at Angus.

Finally Angus starts up again.
"See, first Mum got sick. Heard voices
coming out of the radio, saying she got to
                                        poison Angus,
send Angus to the better place.
She put something in the milk.
Angus got real sick.

Later on, Angus got the sickness same as Mum.
Heard voices saying, 'Do this, do that.'

Don't like hospital. They got the radio
going all the time. Here, it's nice.
Nobody tying you to your bed,
nothing like that."

Angus cleaned his plate, thanked Mum
for the dinner like he always did,
then bent himself through the back door
leaving his full glass of milk
sitting on the table.

A NOTICE IN THE PAPER ANNOUNCED
the grand opening of the new library.

There were balloons and streamers,
                          lemonade and cake.
Miss Griffin, the librarian,
said it'd be the first and last time
we'd get to eat in the library.
She takes care of those books
like they're her own children.

Our old library was one room
on the second floor of the city hall.
Now we've got two whole floors
and rows of empty shelves
that will eventually get filled with books.

I got a new library card
with my name typed on it
and a metal piece in the bottom corner
stamped with a string of numbers.

Constable Pettit showed up
sweating in his Mountie uniform
and helped the mayor cut the ribbon.

When he stayed for cake, I waited
between some shelves, watched him talk
to Mrs. Phillips and Mrs. Liddle. I wanted
to ask a question to the one person
who knows everything that goes on in town.

Finally I went up to him.
"Constable Pettit? Have you seen my dad?"
                    I said, looking way up.
And he looked down at me, then
he looked all around the room and back
down at me, one big hand under his plate,
the other hand holding his fork.
            "Yeah. I've seen your dad."

"You know if he's got plans to leave town?" I asked.

He chewed on his bottom lip, making his moustache
squirm like a caterpillar.
"Well," he said, taking a big breath.
"Haven't seen him in a while.
But all I can say is,
            I haven't seen him leave."

I know my dad.
And he would never leave town
without telling me first.

I've started a list
of things I want to remember about Dad.

1. When I came up just past Dad's knees
   I'd climb into his lap, try to pick up his fingers,
   his big, hairy hands.

2. He'd go hunting every fall, bring home pheasants.
   I thought they were so pretty, was so sad
   they were dead.

3. Dad brought home a puppy the Christmas Eve
   I was seven. That was Prince.

4. Dad would yell at Prince in his deep voice.
   But Prince would follow him everywhere.

5. On my ninth birthday Dad drove from Estevan
   through a thunderstorm so he could get home
   for my cake and ice cream.
   "I'd never miss your birthday, Em," he said.

ME AND ANGUS TOOK THE TRACTOR.
To Wang's Grocery.
Before we could open the front door,
Mei's three little sisters came flying out
of that store, all wanting to clamber up
                              on the tractor.
Mei's dad came out grinning,
shook Angus's hand, said hello to me
with a little bow.

Mr. Wang makes it his business
to treat every customer like a king.
It's how he gets along
with the powerful people in town.

Angus looked like a giant
as he lifted those little girls up,
then had them switch seats
until all three got a turn on each seat.

Mei came out and stood by me.
I could tell she wanted
to climb up on the tractor, too,
so I suggested it.

We sat up there and talked while Mr. Wang
opened the door wide for Angus
and got him everything on our list.

When we left, the whole family,
including Mei's mum and auntie,
stood at the door and waved. Her mum
said to me, "You come visit Mei.
She tells me you're a good friend."

I smiled, hoping Mum would let me.

THAT MARINER ROCKET MADE IT ALL THE WAY
                                                    to Mars
and sent back pictures.
Scientists think Mars is covered with canals
that maybe Martians dug once, but the pictures
show no sign of life.

One thing color TV's good for is to see
pictures of the red planet. I called Mum over
and wanted to run out and call Angus,
but then I remembered what he said
about hearing voices through the radio,
                              and I let it go.

CLOUD BUILT UP ALL DAY IN THE HEAT.
By five o'clock a thunderhead, dark and rumbling,
was high in the sky, moving closer.
Big raindrops started to fall, slammed
into the dry ground, left craters
                              in the dirt.
Angus was standing out in the flax.
I stood at the edge of the yard
beside the clothesline. Suddenly
the hair on my arms stood on end.
Angus shouted at me
                    to run inside fast as I could.
Lightning.

Sure enough, the sky let go. I watched
through the big front window as the ink blue sky
threw down its rain so thick I couldn't see
across to town. Thunder came so close
behind the lightning
it must have been right on top of us.

Angus stood on the porch till the storm passed,
till sunlight broke in a slant
                        through the clouds.

"No sign of hail," he said.
"That's good," Mum said.
"It's a good crop, real good crop," he said.
"Don't want hail."

ANGUS DROVE ME TO DR. PHILLIPS' OFFICE
while Mum walked. He sawed off my cast.
But now I can't walk
except with my left foot on tiptoe.

Dr. Phillips says in Regina
there's a man who'll build up
my shoe so I can walk normally.
Made me wonder how long it would take
to drive to Regina
on a tractor.

I'M LIKE A TABLE WITH UNEVEN LEGS,
one where the milk sloshes
out of the glasses every time
the table gets bumped.

Angus rummaged around in the shed
and came out with a piece of lumber
under his arm.

"Stand on this," he said. Went back into the shed,
came out with a thicker piece of wood.

"Angus is gonna fix your shoe
so you can walk," he said.

I'm trying to think what I'd be like
if my mum tried to poison me
like Angus's mum did him. Wonder
if I'd go around talking about myself
like I was someone else.

ANGUS SAID HE NEEDED A CERTAIN MACHINE
to cut the wood right. Can't remember
what it's called. He walked over to the mental hospital
with my shoe and his block of wood.

I watched him disappear into the caragana bushes.

Little while later Angus came back,
spoke to Mum. Mum agreed to let me go
but only if she came along.

I held my breath
as we walked through the caragana bushes.
Quiet. A cricket chirping. Someone
                                    mowing the lawn.

Angus opened the door to a big brick building.
We sat on chairs in the hallway.
I stared at the high ceiling, green walls.
The chairs were old and reminded me
of a train station.

Heard the sound of a radio
way off down the hall. Someone
pounding out a song on the piano,
                    then playing it again. And again.
Someone else talking fast without stopping.
Two nurses walking a man down the hall
who wore a jacket that tied his arms tight to his sides.

Mum sat with her arms crossed,
stared straight ahead.

Then a door opened. Mum jumped.

Mr. Sidloski was a small man
with gray hair and glasses. Wore a white coat.
His son Graham got his picture in the paper
at least once every winter
                    for playing hockey.
Mr. Sidloski smiled,
said he wanted to meet the people
Angus spoke so highly about.
He shook Mum's hand.
Then he shook mine.

He measured my two legs,
had me stand with my left foot
on different-sized blocks.
                When he got it right,
he compared the block with the one Angus
brought over. "By golly," he said,
"I think we can make this work."

Mr. Sidloski took Angus's block and my shoe
and some big goggles and said, "Come on, Angus.
Let's have you do this."
                    And they left the room together.

About half an hour later, they came back.

Wearing my built-up shoe, I walked
With Mum and Angus through the green
hallway and out the door. We passed
the man mowing the lawn, passed
through the caragana bushes.
                    And I broke ahead.
I ran home. Didn't stop
until I'd slapped the side
of our white house.

ANGUS WAS WAIST DEEP IN THE MUSTARD,
pulling up a few stalks.

"Angus?" I said. "Where
did you learn how to farm?"
I followed him back to the porch
steps, where he was slamming the stalks
against the white boards.

"Foster family — Selkes. Live out
near Kisbey. Good people.
                    Real good people."

"Do you ever see them?" I asked.
He was looking close at the porch boards
to see if anything crawled out of the plants.

"They came up to hospital for awhile."

"Well, now that you're out,
do you want to see them again?"

He picked up a tiny, crawling thing,
examined it, shook his head,
                    looked up.
"People just want to go back
to the way things used to be.
That place is gone.
It's never coming back."

WHEAT BOARD PUT OUT A CALL.
They're selling our wheat
to the Soviet Union.
Now our quiet summer
is bustling like harvest time.
Every farmer around is hurrying
to get their two-year-old wheat
out of the bins, sell seven bushels to the acre.

Mum dipped into our food money
to buy a new battery for the two-ton.
Says when we get paid for the wheat
we'll fix the car.

We augured out our bins, filled the truck.
While Angus drove it to the elevator,
Mum and I swept one bin clean, got ready
to augur out another, fill the truck again
when Angus came back.

Some people wonder why, with the Cold War
going on, Wheat Board's selling
                              to communists.
Newspaper called it feeding the enemy.

But most farmers are too busy
thinking about how this wheat sale
is going to get them out of debt
to worry about who they're selling to.

Slipped out early this morning,
walked down to the El Rancho.
Lots of grain trucks pulling into town.

Louise was working the desk.
"Sorry, hon," she said. "He left
for the railyard real early this morning.
Everybody's working
to get all that grain shipped out of here."

Then it hit me. If I'd gone with Angus
to deliver the grain, I might have
                        run into Dad.

Louise said, "I gave him your last note,"
and I shook my head a little
to come back to where I was standing.
All I could say was,
"Can I leave another one?"

"Sure, hon," she said and found some paper
for me. I wrote,
Dad,
We're selling our wheat. Got some money.
Please come home.
                    Emmie
While I was writing she went on,
                         "I wouldn't go
down there right now if I was you.
Grain trucks running everywhere and trains
pulling in and out. You go down there,
they'll shoo you off soon's look at you."

I slid the note to her.
"Now, Cal told me your name — Emily?"

"Emaline," I said.

"Nice to meet you, Emaline. Hey, I see
you got your cast off." She looked hard
at my leg, at my shoe.
                    "Man," she said,
"it must've been real messed up."

I PUSHED THROUGH THE HEAVY DOORS
and out into the sun, blinked back
        the light.
Glanced down at my leg.

It was just a little shriveled-up stick
compared to my other leg. Looked like
somebody'd marked all over it with a fat
                              red pen.
My shoe that I was so happy about
felt heavy and clunky. And just like that,
I felt ugly.

I started walking. When I got as far
the railroad tracks, I looked way off in the distance,
and I could see a train coming toward town.

I looked the other way, squinted
at the grain elevators all wavy
in the heat, and the line of trucks
heaped with grain, churning up dust
behind their wheels.

I kept looking for Dad, wanting
to walk down there and find him, tell him
about our crops, pull him home.

But I'd seen my leg the way it really was.
And I was afraid Dad
would think it was ugly, too.

JAMIE AND JOEY ARE SPENDING THEIR SUMMER
blowing up gopher holes
with firecrackers left over from July.

Joey came over to show off
his string of thirty-two gopher tails,
and it was just like Joey that he ended up
ripping through Angus's suitcase
and blankets in the shed.
Joey picked up Angus's caboose,
danced around with it,

was still dancing
when Angus showed up, roaring.
                          Ripped that caboose
right out of Joey's hand.

Me and Angus watched Joey run home
like he was being chased by a monster.

JAMIE OFFERED TO BLOW UP GOPHER HOLES
             at our place for money.
Had half a dozen Black Cat firecrackers in his fist.
Opened up his hand. He stepped back
when Angus came close.

I looked. Angus looked.
Then Angus took us into the shed,
pulled an old milk crate off a shelf.
                          Heavy wooden box.
Sent Jamie to find a Y-shaped stick.
Sent me inside to put peanut butter
on a lettuce leaf.

We walked out to a spot of hardly any grass,
where there were lots of gopher holes.
                          Near the edge
of one hole, Angus tilted the milk crate.
The Y-stick held up one side.
He tied twine to the stick, told me
to put the lettuce on the ground
under the tilting crate, gave the end
of the twine to Jamie.

Jamie held out his firecrackers.
"Don't need those," said Angus.

Me and Jamie lay on our stomachs on the ground.
We had to be still. Not a sound.
Angus filled up a bucket with water.
Poured it down the hole.

We waited.

Pretty soon a gopher came out,
                              looked around,
went for the lettuce. Jamie
snapped the crate down. Angus
pounced on the crate, held it
with his giant hands.

Angus said, "Sometimes they don't come out
first time, just come up by the other hole.
Poke up their heads and look at you."

We slipped a square of old screen
under the crate. Stapled the edges tight.
Turned the crate over.

Gopher was in there, peeping
and squealing and wet. Angus put the crate
                              in Jamie's arms.
"Keen," said Jamie, his eyes bugged out.

"You want him?" said Angus.
"Yeah," Jamie said.

"You'll have to build him a bigger cage.
Put some straw down. Put in a old shoebox
for his bedroom. He likes it dark," said Angus.

"What do I feed him?"

"Potato peelings, carrot peelings.
Root parts of weeds and grass.
Don't forget water."

"Thanks," said Jamie.

Now we hear him hammering
down at his place, working
on that cage.

If Joey's jealous for his own gopher pet,
he hasn't come around.

HEARD COYOTES IN THE NIGHT
from my open window.
Far away.
One pack calling,
another answering.
Young ones yipping
along with deeper voices.
Smell of wood smoke
on the night air.
A full moon.
Their high whines.
Their wild choir.

SOMEONE TRIED TO BURN DOWN
our shed last night.
Angus smelled smoke,
heard someone stepping
on gravel.

He put the fire out
with the garden hose.
Good thing there was no wind
or that shed would have taken off.

The burned place is a hole
big enough for me to crawl through.

I told Mum
we've got to find a better spot
for Angus to sleep
before the summer's over.
Maybe our back room
by the canning cupboard.

I think Angus knows
who started the fire.
But far as I know,
he's not saying.

Mei asked if I could come for a visit,
and this time Mum said yes.

I was glad to see Mei. Her mum and dad
looked at my leg, the scars,
my elevator shoe. Her auntie
took me upstairs where they live
and into the kitchen,
where she started to feed me. Noodles,
                              spring rolls.

Mei showed me her room —
one big room she shares with her little sisters.
Curtains hang from the ceiling,
                              but it's not private.
Mei's sisters, Lilli and Lin,
sat outside the curtain around Mei's bed,
desk and dresser. They giggled.

Little Caroline wandered in and out,
pulling the curtain. Mei
picked up Caroline and tried
to chase Lilli and Lin away
but they always came back,
like twittering birds
to a telephone line.

LILLI, LIN AND MEI GO SWIMMING
at the Souris pool three times a week.
They hung on my arms, wanted me
                              to come along.

Mei walked home with me
and I asked Mum, reminded her it's free.
Rotary Club pays for the pool every summer
so kids can have a place to go.
                    But I hadn't gone
because I was afraid all the kids
would point at my leg, and because
I'd have a hard time walking
after I took my shoe off. But Mei
and her sisters kept asking.
                    And Mum said yes.

The cold water felt so good.
Once I was in, I moved like a fish,
                    kicking and squirming,
no heavy shoe to lug around. I turned somersaults
in the water. I floated on my back
and raced underwater,
like nothing had happened
to change me forever.

MY BIRTHDAY'S ON THE 14TH,
so Mum asked me if I'd like to have a party
and who I'd like to invite.
I thought for awhile, then I made four invitations,
took them around after supper.

I gave one to Angus, and he looked it all over.
"A party?" he said, like he'd never
got a birthday invitation in his life.

I took one to Miss Tollofsen,
who was standing like a tower
on her green lawn, watering her flowers,
and she smiled at my drawing of a cake
                        and candles, balloons
and a dog and cat sitting on each side of the cake.

I walked up to Wangs', where I handed Mei
an invitation. Mei showed her mum and auntie
the picture I had drawn, and her auntie
said, "My, you very talented girl."
And they grinned and said yes,
                        Mei could come.

Then I took an invitation to Dad.

I'D NEVER BEEN TO THE EL RANCHO AT NIGHT.
I'd planned to walk in and spot Dad
in the restaurant eating his dinner, chicken
                              and mashed potatoes,
and it would be darker in the restaurant
so he wouldn't see my leg right away
but see me first, me and my party invitation.

Louise was behind the desk.
Outside I could hear the clanging sound
of signal lights. I could hear
a train rumbling on the tracks.

"You just missed him, hon,"
                              she said quietly.

"Well, can you give him this invitation?
For my birthday party."

And Louise said, "Didn't he tell you?
                              Cal checked out.
He's working one of those trains going west.
Checked out a couple hours ago."

This wasn't right at all. I turned around
to look into the restaurant. Dad
was supposed to be eating dinner. Alone.
I would walk up shyly and say his name.
He'd stand up smiling, so glad
                    to see me at last,
throw his arms around me.
He would take the invitation and say,
"Of course, I'd never
               miss your birthday, Em."

I pushed my way into the hot evening,
the signal bells banging in my ears.
                    The tail end of that train
was just pulling through the crossing.
I looked up as the caboose rocked past,
raised my hand like I always do to wave
at the caboose man sitting in the window.
I could see his dark hair and bushy eyebrows.

I was waving goodbye
to Dad.

MUM MADE A DEVIL'S FOOD CAKE.
I made sandwiches with tuna,
mayonnaise and lettuce,
cut them into triangles
and arranged them on a plate.
I cut carrot sticks and celery,
filled the celery with peanut butter,
sprinkled raisins on the peanut butter.
Mum made pink lemonade.

Mei arrived precisely at 2:30. Angus
was early and sat like a tree, his arms
                           drooping like branches
over the sides of his chair.
Miss Tollofsen drove over. At the door,
she explained how her mother had always told her,
arrive to a party five minutes late,
just in case your hostess isn't ready.

I passed around paper party plates
and matching napkins. Then I passed
the sandwiches. Mum poured
                           the lemonade.

Miss Tollofsen got Angus talking
about how he used to go to a one-room school
near Kisbey. She even knew where it was.
She got Mei talking, too, but I mostly listened.

Seemed like I was the only one
who was thinking there was somebody
missing
from my party.

MUM BROUGHT OUT THE CAKE,
twelve candles lit and dripping.
                    I blew them out
and opened my presents.

Mum's present to me
was a transistor radio with an earphone.
I hadn't expected such a big present.
Mei gave me stationery,
and Miss Tollofsen gave me a book
on how to draw animals.

I opened Angus's present last, fumbled
with the paper and tape
until something heavy
fell into my lap.

His caboose.

Evening, I sat on the steps with Angus.
We watched the sunset. All the colors
Angus sees. Red and orange,
blue, yellow. Bit of green.

We watched the fields as far as we could see.
Bright as gold in the setting sun.
When Mum finally called me in,
I left Angus still watching the sky.

Into the night I lay
looking at Angus's caboose
where I'd set it on my windowsill,
and imagined Dad's train
getting smaller and smaller
going west across Saskatchewan
till it was just a pencil mark
on a giant piece of paper,
and Dad's face so clear in my head
from that second I saw him —
the lines in his forehead
not crunched together anymore,
                              but smooth,
and a look of happiness on his face.

EVERYWHERE YOU WALK NOW
turns up grasshoppers. Put one foot
on the ground, they fly up
in a fountain of bugs. They buzz
and bang into the windows.
Drive anywhere, and they catch
in the grill. Then you've got the smell
of toasted grasshopper.

Angus says
it's not as bad as some years
since we had that rain. Grasshoppers
love a drought. But still,
they help themselves to the grain
before it's harvested.

Don't know yet
how they take to mustard
and flax.

"ANGUS?" I BEGAN. I FOLLOWED HIM
                    out to the fields.
"Do you ever think of your mum?"

"Sometimes. Used to be all the time.
Even after she got locked up in hospital,
Angus'd see her at night, coming
                    with poison.
Sit up screaming.
Foster mum would come in, say
                    Angus gotta forgive.
Forgive and let her go.

But Angus didn't know how
                    to forgive,
so in my mind I put her in a basket.
Put balloons on the basket.
In my mind. And I let her rise
                    up into the sky,
till she was a wee speck.
Did that every day. Every now and again
I have to put her back in that basket,
send her to the sky.
But not very often now. Not much."

I stood there in mustard up to my waist
and stared at Angus, my mouth
wide open at what
he'd just said.

I LIFTED UP MY MATTRESS
to look at the pencil marks on my wall.
All the days Dad was gone.
They go halfway down the length
of my bed.

I set the mattress back down
without making another mark.

Then I wrote a couple more things about Angus.

Seven. He put his mum in a basket, let her go.

Eight. He said "I."

Meeka

First day of school,
I caught up with Mei and her sisters
at the edge of the schoolyard,
waited with them till we were called in.
I wore a new dress
Mum bought me in Regina —
red and black plaid,
white collar and cuffs
and a black bow at my throat.

Teachers came out one at a time
and called their grades in.
After Miss Tollofsen called
                    the grade sixes,
the only ones left in the schoolyard
were the grade sevens and eights.

Finally Mr. Liddle,
        vice-principal and grade seven teacher,
came out, squinted and frowned at us.

"Grade sevens — raise your hands!" he called,
as he raised his own hand high.
We raised our hands.

"You're all grade sevens?" he asked, leaning
forward to get a better look at us.

"Yes!" we called back, nodding.

"No little lost souls who missed the call
                                for grade two?"

"No!" we called.

Jamie held up Joey's hand. "He did!"

"Shut up," said Joey.

Mr. Liddle's frown relaxed into a smile.
                                He waved us in,
and we followed him into our new classroom.

I wanted to tell Mum all about my day,
especially how Mr. Liddle stood on his desk
with a flashlight and dinner plate
to show the earth's rotation around the sun.

I crossed the yard, took the steps two at a time.
                              Opened the door.

Mum sat slumped in her chair, dish towel in her hand,
like she'd just got punched in the stomach.
Someone was talking on the radio,
then a song started. She didn't look up
when I came in the front door.

"We got cheated," she said in nearly a whisper.
"It was just on the news. Wheat Board
                              sold our wheat too low."

"What do you mean, too low?"

"For years Wheat Board wouldn't buy our wheat.
There was a world-wide glut, they said,
too much wheat.
Price was rock bottom for wheat.

When the Soviets wanted to buy our wheat,
they told the Wheat Board
they had plenty of wheat in their fields.
Didn't have any. The Reds lied.

"Wheat Board sold our wheat for half the price
they should have sold it for," whispered Mum.

"Guess it's good we're planting mustard
and flax now," I said.

When Angus came in, Mum shut off the radio.

My leg ached. I ate supper and went to my room.

MY LEG KNEW THE WEATHER
was about to change. Storm
came through last night.
Wind and cloud and icy rain.

Angus says what you don't harvest
in August, you'll harvest in October.

Guess we'll harvest in October.

ANGUS, I FOUND OUT,
doesn't understand jokes.
I said, "Angus, did you hear about the man
who was walking down the street
and turned into a drugstore?"
And Angus just stood there
in the middle of the garden holding
                                    a giant squash,
waiting for me to finish the story.

I said, "That's it. Like the prince
that got turned into a frog, this man
turned into a drugstore."
                          And Angus
shook his head.
"That can't happen," he said.

But one evening at supper, we started talking
about how me and Mum went shopping
                          that day at Wang's.
We stood at the check-out holding our baskets
while Mrs. Torkleson, in front of us,
took apart her handbag, looking
for her change purse.

She took out keys
and red lipstick
and hand cream,
set them one by one on the counter
with cigarettes
and a lighter
and a pair of pliers.

Angus about fell off his chair laughing
                              over that pair of pliers
coming out of Mrs. Torkleson's purse.

IF MR. LIDDLE CATCHES YOU WRITING A NOTE,
you have to read it aloud to the entire class.

Today during silent reading, I got out my list
about Dad and started writing.

6. Dad could wink his eyes just like the red
   signal lights at train crossings.

7. I learned to count past one hundred
   by counting train cars with Dad
   whenever we got stopped at crossings.

8. Whenever I dressed up in Mum's
   dress and shoes, he called me Princess.
   I'd sing, "I'm Daddy's princess."

I felt a finger tap my shoulder. I looked up.
Mr. Liddle stood over me like a skyscraper.
                              Held his palm out.
I turned the paper over to him.

The whole class looked up from their books
                              to watch.

"Make her read it, Mr. Liddle!"
It was Joey, of course.

I looked straight ahead at nothing
while Mr. Liddle held the paper.
Then he folded it in half with a crease
                    and handed it back to me.

"Perhaps you can do this at home," he said,
one hand on my shoulder.

It would have been easier
if he hadn't laid his big, warm hand
so gently on my shoulder.

As it was, I put my face into my book,
but I couldn't stop the tears
that dropped onto the page.

I WASN'T OFF THE SCHOOL GROUNDS
when Joey grabbed my book with the paper in it
and held it high over my head.

"Who's this love note to?"

"Give it back," I warned, "or you'll be sorry."

"Sorry. Gimpy says I'll be sorry,"
Joey called in a high whiny voice,
waving my book around.

I punched him in the stomach, then grabbed my book.

Mr. Liddle waded through the crowd, saw
Joey bent double, me in front of him
and kids crowded in a circle around us.

"Emaline, did you hit him?" Mr. Liddle asked.
His low voice echoed in my ears like a bell.

I nodded, and he let out
a loud sigh.
                        "Come with me."

I walked ahead of Mr. Liddle up the steps
and back into the classroom.

"Sit down, Emaline," he said.

I sat myself down on one of the wooden seats
at the front of the class.

Mr. Liddle brought his chair around
to sit in front of me. He crossed his legs
and folded his hands in his lap.

My stomach tightened up like a fist
wondering what he was going to do.

"Please don't call my mum," I pleaded.
I lowered my head and sobbed quietly
as Mr. Liddle watched me.

Mr. Liddle tipped back in his chair, reached
for a piece of paper on his desk, handed it to me.
"Perhaps you'll be interested in this."

Student Volunteer Opportunity

*The Souris Animal Shelter requires volunteers from
students grades seven and above, one afternoon per
week or on Saturdays. Responsibilities include
cleaning kennels, feeding dogs and cats, acting as
companion to injured or abandoned animals.
Teacher recommendation preferred.*

Call Pat Spiske — 842-3653.

Mr. Liddle watched me read. Then he said,
"If you'd like, I'll call Mrs. Spiske
and recommend you."

And here I'd been thinking
how this was just the second day of school
and already my new teacher was going to think
I'm a troublemaker.

I SHOWED UP AT THE ANIMAL SHELTER
on Saturday.
Mrs. Spiske showed me the cat and kitten room,
how to clean their cages. Said they needed
to be picked up and petted,
especially the kittens.

We went out back to the dog cages.
Lots of dogs. I tried to remember
which ones were fierce
and which were tame. In all the barking,
I didn't hear everything Mrs. Spiske said to me.

Near the door was a big cage
with its door wide open, a white and brown
sled dog inside, one brown eye, one blue.
"We don't know her name," said Mrs. Spiske.
"We just call her Meeka.
D'Arcy Pettit found her on the highway

                                        at a crash,
brought her here. We think her owner got killed.
She doesn't take to people now,
just sits in the shadows."

While I put clean newspaper
on the floor of each cat cage,
I carried a cat on my shoulder.
I filled the dogs' bowls
and replaced their water.
Then I went inside Meeka's cage
and sat down a little ways from her.
She lay with her chin on her paws.
Only her ears twitched
to show she knew I was there.

THE SKY CLEARED, CLOUDED,
snowed small, hard flakes
and cleared again. It's cold at night,
but Angus says that shouldn't hurt the crop.
Soon as we get a stretch of dry days, we'll harvest.

Last night I woke up not knowing
what time it was. Got a drink of water,
started back to bed.
　　　　　Peeked out the window.

What I saw
looked like curtains of light, green and red,
like scarves waving across the sky.

And then something else caught my eye.
It was Angus, his arms stretched out,
and Angus was at the edge of the yard
dancing beneath the northern lights.

MEEKA RAISED HER HEAD
when I walked into her cage,
then put her chin back down
on her paws.

Back home,
I got out my paper and pencils,
started drawing her like that.
Chin on her paws, ears
alert and forward.

Mr. Liddle made a seating chart
and we all got moved around.
Me and Mei had been sitting together.
In the new seating chart, I was to sit
beside Jamie Record.

"At least he didn't make you sit by Joey," Mei said,
and she's right.

I'd never noticed before
how fidgety Jamie gets
when he's been inside too long.

Comes into the classroom
after the last bell has rung.
Springs out of his seat
at the bells for lunch and recess.

Says he just can't stand too much roof
over his head. "My mum says
I'm a born farmer," says Jamie,
all while his foot and knee
are bouncing under his desk.

MEEKA WALKED OUT OF HER CAGE,
followed me into the cat and kitten room,
lay on the floor while I cleaned the cages.
She sniffed one of the kittens
that romped on the floor
while I changed the paper in its cage.
              The kitten, Tiger
I call him, turned around,
stuck out his little pink nose,
touched Meeka's big black one.

NIGHT COMES EARLY NOW.
Tonight I took out my drawings of Prince
and my drawing of Meeka.
                              Drew Meeka again
nose to nose with a kitten.

When I put my drawings away
and turned out the light,
darkness rushed in like water. Not even a moon out.
                    Just clouds streaking across the stars,
                        stretched out long
and smoothed by the wind.

Only light was in my head,
thinking of Dad riding in a caboose
at the end of a train a mile long,
and the light from his window
a little yellow square
going west toward the sea.

HARVEST, AT LAST.
Southwest wind. Almost like summer again.
I'm behind the steering wheel of the two-ton,
sitting on implement manuals to make me taller,
so I can see over the wheel. Angus
built up the pedals with blocks of wood
so I can reach them with my feet.

I have to drive the truck alongside the tractor
that Angus is driving, pulling the combine.
If I fall behind or rush ahead, the grain
will fall on the ground or on the truck cab,
not in the box where we want it.

After awhile Mum takes over.
She's steadier than I am.
We harvest as long as the light will let us.

Sunday, Jamie comes by, offers to help.
Angus puts him to work, but then
his dad spots him in the field with me
and Angus, and red-faced Harry
hauls him home, shouting.

The harvest will last for days. Monday,
Mum will drive the two-ton until I'm home
from school, and then I'll drive till dark.
We'll fill our empty bins.

Me, I'm filled with the wind, sky, smell
of ground, harvest dust in my nose,
my lungs, the land in my skin and hair.

I'm land, I'm sky.
I'm Saskatchewan.

VIDA RECORD CALLED MUM
three times today, said,
*Think of your own safety. Think
of your neighbors.*
Tonight, Harry came over,
said he wouldn't leave until Mum agreed
to send Angus back to hospital.
Says we don't need him now.
Farm work's over. And Harry
                    didn't leave
until Angus stomped in the back door,
got himself a drink of water
at the kitchen sink.

Harry said, "Something's bound to happen.
You're putting us all in danger, Clarice.
We got a right to our own peace of mind."

Mum said,
"May be a dangerous man about.
But it's not Angus."

MUM CAME EARLY
to pick me up from the shelter,
said she'd chat with Mrs. Spiske
while I finished feeding the animals.

I didn't think anything about it.
Meeka followed me around
as usual to all the cages. She's
my little shadow, Mrs. Spiske says.

When I got finished, Meeka
followed me to the door.
"Well, Meeka, you have a new family,"
Mrs. Spiske said. And my heart sank.
Who was taking her home?

Mum smiled. "It'll be good
to have a dog around the place again."
Turned out Mum came early
to sign the papers. I hugged Mum hard.
Then I hugged Meeka.

MEEKA DIDN'T REALLY WANT TO LEAVE
the shelter, go out into the night.
I had to carry her to the car.
She didn't want to get in the car either.
When Mum opened the door
she stuck out her front legs, and her hind legs
pushed backwards against my arm.
But I got her in and I sat with her there
in the back seat,
next to the bag of dog food Mrs. Spiske gave us.
Scratched her behind the ears, chatted softly to her
the whole ride home.

I LET MEEKA SNIFF AROUND OUTSIDE
the house, then I brought her in.

Angus's face lit up when she came in the door.
He squatted down and petted her
and talked to her in a quiet voice
about her one blue eye,
her black nose, white paws,
her pointy, alert ears.

I said, "What color's she got
                    around her, Angus?"

And Angus said, scratching under
Meeka's chin, "Mostly yellow.
Yellow's a good color. She's happy.
She's home."

MUM THOUGHT MEEKA
with her heavy coat might get too hot
sleeping in the house overnight.
Angus said she'd be fine outside,
being mostly husky, after all. I said
if she was going to spend the night outside,
                              I'd better tie her up
so she didn't get confused and wander off,
so someone wouldn't mistake her for a coyote
                                    and shoot her.

After supper, me and Angus
went out to the shed and dug around for rope.
We tied her to the back porch post,
gave her water and food
and went to bed.

She was fine till about midnight,
when she started yipping and howling.
Not the crisp three-note howl the coyotes make,
but a howl that wandered all over the place,
like some sick and dying cow.

Three times I stuck my head out my window.
The October air hit me cold in the face.
"Meeka," I called. "It's okay.
Don't cry, honey."

Two minutes later, there she'd go again.
It was an awful howl.

I guess animals are like people.
Some can sing, some can't.

WE GOT SOME SLEEP
at last. When I woke,
I remembered Meeka, looked out.
She wasn't on the end of her rope.

Seemed everyone was still sleeping.
I could hear Mum softly snoring
in her room. I tiptoed downstairs,
walked through the kitchen
to Angus's room, where his door
sat open just a crack. Peeked in.

There was Angus asleep on his cot,
his arm hanging down to the floor
where Meeka slept curled up
under his enormous hand.

WIND ROARED OVER THE LAND TODAY.
Warm wind. Pulled the clouds out
long and thin. Blew the October leaves
clean off the trees. From the window
of our classroom, I could see those clouds
being stretched, leaves swirling.

Outside, we nearly had to yell to be heard.
Wind rattled the windows of Haig School
and we leaned into the wind home.
Mr. Liddle says there's going to be a change
in the weather.
A big change.

Joey

We stayed after school Friday
to decorate for the Halloween party.
Each class was in charge of an event —
bobbing for apples,
haunted house, hot dog and cider supper.
Our classroom was going to be
                    Frankenstein's Workshop.

We draped sheets over the rows of desks,
where bowls of cold spaghetti and peeled grapes,
                    and globs of wiggly Jell-O
would feel like eyeballs, and guts, and brains.
Some of us would hide under the desks
and grab people's legs as they passed.

Joey bounced around and got in people's way.
Even Mr. Liddle couldn't keep him on a project
for long. Finally Joey announced
he was going home.
We barely looked up as he left.

Miss Tollofsen poked her head in the door.
"Radio says a blizzard's on its way. Wind's
already shifted to north."

Mr. Liddle asked, "Anyone walking home?"
Mei, Jamie and I raised our hands.
"Make sure you go soon. We'll take care
of the rest," Mr. Liddle said.

But we forgot, trying to finish
hanging the black and orange streamers
in the doorway. By the time
we gathered our coats and started for home,
it was already dark.

We walked together
and talked, me and Mei and Jamie.
I asked Mei what she was going to be
                    for Halloween.
Alice in Wonderland, she said. Caroline,
her littlest sister, was going to dress up as a bunny,
so they could be Alice and the White Rabbit.

Jamie was going to be Zorro.
I didn't want to tell, but finally let out
that I planned to be the Tin Man
                    from *The Wizard of Oz*.
"How are you going to do that?" they asked
as we walked along the narrow sidewalk, the wind
picking up with every step we took.

Truth is, I'd been collecting oatmeal cartons
for months, been painting them silver,
made a cardboard cone hat, and I planned
to bring along a little oil tin
from the shed.

We said goodbye to Mei
in front of her store.
Snow had started to blow in slants
and the temperature was falling by the minute.

Up ahead I could see headlights
and Jamie's dad's white truck
coming toward us. As it passed, I saw
Harry driving, and a very big man beside him.

I flipped around as the taillights of the truck
disappeared in blowing snow,
headed through town.

"That's your dad's truck," I said to Jamie.
"Did you see who was in there?"

"Looked like Angus," he said.

WIND WHISTLED AROUND US.
We pulled our coats tighter, walked
the rest of the way in silence, snow
                          stinging my legs
through my woolen tights, my heart
pounding through my ears.

Mrs. Record stormed out onto her porch.
"Jamie!" she called. She was just a dark form
moving behind the thickening snow.
"Is Joey with you?"

"No, Mum. He left early," Jamie called back.

"What???" she yelled.

"He left early!"

The alarm that rang in my head
on seeing Angus
        riding in Harry's truck
rang even louder.

And still I couldn't imagine how long
        that night would be.

I BLEW IN THE FRONT DOOR.
Meeka sniffed the snow
stuck to my legs.

"There you are," Mum sighed. "Storm's
blowing in fast.
Run out and tell Angus it's suppertime."

"Angus isn't in the shed," I told her,
my voice shaking, my stomach in knots.

Then I told her what I'd seen — the truck,
Harry, Angus inside.
That Joey was missing, too.

Mum's hands flew up to both sides
of her face. She paced in a circle.
"Harry Record!
        What is that man thinking?"
She picked up the phone.

D'Arcy Pettit's switchboard was busy.
Busy at Records' house, too.

Mum ran to the door, looked out.

"Can't see hand in front of face," she declared,
and shut the door.

Our walls popped and cracked
as the temperature fell outside. A gust
                                    of wind
hit the house so hard I could feel the blow.

Except for one light over the kitchen sink,
we sat in the dark. Neither of us got up
to turn on a light.

Mum picked up the phone again.
                    "Line's dead.
Not even a dial tone," she said.

MEEKA PACED THE FLOOR,
                    lay down, groaned.
Got up, walked through Angus's room,
came back, lay down, groaned.

I saw the truck over and over in my head,
coming toward me, saw the faces
behind the windshield, red lights
disappearing in the distance.

Mum said, "Well, we can't just sit here."

I said, "Maybe Mrs. Record's got through
                    to Constable Pettit.
I could go over and see."

I didn't think Mum would agree
to me striking out in a blizzard.
But all she said was,
"Take Meeka."

MUM HELPED GET ME READY.
I put on long underwear.
Pants and sweater. Coat, scarf, toque, mitts.
I tied Meeka's rope to her collar.
Mum tied the other end around my waist.
Handed me a flashlight.

Outside, I pointed myself toward Records'
and started to walk. In the light
of the flashlight I could see nothing
                                but slanting snow.
I could feel Meeka tugging at the rope.

I never knew how big our field could be.
I had to walk slowly on the uneven ground
as my legs sank deeper and deeper into snow.
I pulled Meeka close, and counted.

When we were seven, me and Joey and Jamie
counted the steps from their house to mine.
                                Two hundred and ten.
I've always remembered that.
Now I counted to fifty. Fifty-one. Fifty-two.
I talked to Meeka. Didn't know
if she could hear me through the wind
and snow, me talking behind my scarf.

Sixty-nine, seventy.

I thought things I hadn't thought
in a long time. About Dad — how
he hated to eat peas, how he'd say,
                    "Got no future in 'em,"
like they were a crop.
Eighty-seven.

I thought about Angus
when he first came to us.
Mum saying, "Stay away from him."
Ninety-two.

How he tied up my shoelace.
Ninety-nine. One hundred.

How he taught me to feed mice.
How we buried Prince together.
Hundred eight.

I remembered Miss Tollofsen
going right over to shake his hand.
Hundred eighteen.

The look on his face
when the folks from OK Economy
accused him of stealing that coffee can
full of cash. Hundred twenty-six.

Same look on his face as I saw him
in Harry Record's truck.
Hundred forty-two.

Hundred and fifty. Fifty-one. Fifty-two.
Meeka's right side was covered with snow.
I pulled her to me, brushed her off.
We walked on.

Hundred and seventy.

At a hundred and seventy-two steps
I fell face first into a ditch.

I pushed myself up. Snow in my mitts,
up my sleeves, in my shoes.
Snow pasted to my scarf.
My eyelashes blinking snow.
                    But I knew
I'd reached the road.

Thirty-two steps across the road
I nearly walked right into the side
of D'Arcy Pettit's police car.

MRS. RECORD ANSWERED THE DOOR,
gasped and pulled me inside.
Began to unwrap me.

"Our phone's dead," was all
I could say.

I TOLD CONSTABLE PETTIT
I wanted to show him
where me and Jamie had seen the truck.
He only agreed to take me home.

I sat in the front seat of his cruiser. Meeka
sat in the back, her rope still tied to her.
Constable Pettit brushed the snow
off the car windows with his arm,
then off himself when he got into the car.

The chains on the back tires
went *whomp, whomp, whomp*
as we thudded, slowly,
out of the Records' driveway
and found the road
without losing a tire in the ditch.

Out of the headlights all I could see
was snow, until the wind
let up just for a moment. Then
I could make out our house.
He was about to pull into our yard
when I pointed down the road
                    at a dark form
hunched and walking in the snow.
He drove toward it, then stopped.
Got out.

Snow blew into the car
when he opened his door.
But I could see a giant of a man
pushing through the snow,

a boy in his arms.

ANGUS COLLAPSED HALF FROZEN
onto the police car's back seat,
Joey still in his arms.

Stumbling through the storm,
trying to find his way back, Angus
had scooped Joey up a mile from home.

Mum says that skinny boy
surely would have died
if not for Angus, who held him
until we pulled up to Union Hospital's
front doors, where he pushed out a new burst
of strength and carried Joey inside.

Angus refused to stay for himself,
and so I led him up our front steps,
D'Arcy Pettit holding him straight.
Mum heard the door crash open in the wind,
ran toward the cold and snow rushing
into the house. We took Angus
to the tub, warmed him slowly, fully clothed,
and sat the rest of the night with him
                              looking like a ghost,
face white with frostbite,
eyebrows caked in ice.

It was almost morning by the time
we managed to remove his boots.

AT DAYBREAK
Dr. Phillips arrived,
bandaged Angus's feet and hands, remarked
over and over about his strength.
Said he'd been up all night with Joey,
and Joey would live, but maybe without
                              some toes,
tips of his fingers.

And then Constable Pettit came,
sat alone with Angus on his bed,
took notes, heard Angus tell
who'd driven him past the other side
of town, made him get out, then left him
in a blizzard
on a lonely road.

EVEN BEFORE THE PAPER CAME OUT,
before the snowplows had scraped clean
all the roads, word got out
about the night of the storm,
how Angus saved the life of the boy
whose father had dumped him
outside of town.

People I'd seen driving past our place
                              last spring
to see a crazy man on a tractor drove up again,
this time with casseroles and desserts,
wanting to shake Angus's hand.

And even with some roads still
in bad shape, drifts high as
car windows in places,
a man and woman named Selke,
who'd once had a foster son,
drove over from Kisbey
and rang our doorbell.

SUN BROKE OUT AT LAST ON SUNDAY, THE DAY
so bright it could blind you, the wind
still blowing snow across the ground.
Even so, people continued to come by.
                    Miss Tollofsen
brought shepherd's pie, still warm
from the oven, her dish wrapped
in newspapers and tea towels.

Since it was dinnertime, Mum served it right away.
It was so good, we all said. I asked
could she give me the recipe, and here it is.

Sadie Tollofsen's Shepherd's Pie

Take about a pound of ground beef, and
brown it well in your skillet. While it's
browning, slice up one half of an onion and
two or three carrots. Put those in with the
beef. When the beef is brown and the onions
are soft, spoon off the extra grease. Then
pour in a whole bottle of that chili sauce
that you find next to the ketchup down at
your grocer's. Let that cook while you make
the mashed potatoes. Pour the beef with the
sauce into your casserole dish, and drop the
mashed potatoes over top. Bake it in the
oven 20 minutes or so.

I GOT TO SCHOOL EARLY ON MONDAY.
Found Mr. Liddle in the classroom.
Explained what I wanted to do.
He nodded, said, "Very well, then."

On my way down the hall I passed
Miss Tollofsen outside her door,
her hand on the shoulder of a kid
bundled in toque, scarf, mittens and boots.
                              "Today's a new day,"
she was saying. "That means a fresh start. I hope
you're ready to make a fresh start."

I walked out the boys' entrance to Haig School,
                              down the steps
that Mr. Liddle had already cleared and salted,
then five blocks to the courthouse,
to the arraignment Angus didn't want to attend.

The snow beside the sidewalks was piled up
in some places to my waist.

Inside, it was hot.
A crowd milled around in the hallway.

Constable Pettit called everyone into the courtroom
       with his booming voice.
The crowd filed in. I shuffled toward the door,
saw Jamie and Mrs. Record in front of me.
I slipped to the back of the room.
Harry was escorted in handcuffs
to the prisoner's box.

When Judge Snyder walked in, we all stood up
and sat down again.

Harry was brought up before the judge.
Judge Snyder read the charges,
and I caught this much:
            unlawful confinement
of an individual, criminal mischief, intent
to cause bodily harm, failure to aid...
Judge Snyder said, "How do you plead?"
And Harry said in a voice so loud
it filled the room,
            "Not guilty, sir."

The judge said there would be a trial
for Harry, but until then,
he would be allowed to post bail
and live on his farm.

The arraignment was over. The judge
got up to leave. Everyone got up to leave.
Until his trial came up, Harry
got to stay out of jail, live at home,
drive his truck back and forth past our house
like nothing out of the ordinary
had happened, nothing at all.

HAIG SCHOOL'S HALLOWEEN PARTY
was postponed to Monday night.

Mei and Caroline won the prize
as Alice and the White Rabbit.
I shuffled around in my Tin Man costume
and ran from all the witches.
But there was no Zorro. Jamie didn't come.

ME AND MUM WENT UP TO VISIT JOEY.
I made a card, and I brought the one
our class had signed for him. Mrs. Record
cranked up Joey's bed just like Mum
had once cranked up mine.

Joey was stiller than usual.
He had a tube running from a plastic bag
into his arm, and bandages like baseball mitts
on his hands, so he couldn't bounce
against the walls or swing
from the curtain rods.
But he talked just like Joey.

"Mummy says that Angus man
picked me up out of the snow
where I was getting buried
'cause I fell asleep, but really
I almost died and that giant
Angus man carried me in his giant
arms and kicked open the hospital door
with his giant feet like a kung-fu guy and
that's how come I didn't die."

Mrs. Record told Mum
she couldn't guess why in the world
Harry would plead Not Guilty.
A trial was just going to put Jamie
and me on the spot.
She gave Mum a note
to give to Angus. A thank-you,
she said it was. Said she wished
she could do more, but Harry
was watching her.

I'VE STARTED LETTING MEEKA
walk to school with me.
Each school morning
we head up the road
toward the mental hospital.
I can hear Harry Record
starting his truck, getting ready
to drive into town for coffee
with his buddies.

Sometimes we meet Mei, Lilly and Lin.
Then we climb the steps to school,
and I say goodbye to Meeka, go in.
Hang up my coat and toque.
Walk into the classroom, check
out the window. After a bit,
she heads back home.

Afternoons now I sometimes see her coming,
                              tail wagging,
up the sidewalk to meet me.
Mum says she's got a clock
in her head. Angus says
that makes her a watch dog.
Angus was real proud of himself
for coming up with that one.

Coming home, I can hear Harry
in his machine shed, keeping busy
till his trial comes up. Angus
just minds his own business.
But sometimes in my mind
I have to put Harry in a basket with balloons,
let him float off into the prairie sky.
Figure Angus has to do that, too.

MIDDLE OF THE NIGHT.
I was asleep under piles of covers,
my breath forming clouds in the room.
Angus nudged me awake.

"Emmie! Wake up!" he whispered.
                         "Come outside!"

I opened my eyes, saw only his shape
in the black room.

I put on pants and a sweater
over the longjohns I was sleeping in
and stumbled downstairs. Put on coat,
                              toque, mitts.
Meeka wagged her tail, licked my nose
as I bent to tie my shoes. Mum came out,
put on her coat. Angus
led us out the back door.

I held onto the porch rails
until I was down the steps
                    and onto the snowy ground.

I looked up then, turned around and around.
Colors, stretched out like scarves,
waved and shimmered all over the sky.

Mum said, "Oh, my."

I held out my arms
and twirled, my head back,
trying to take it all in.

Meeka ran in circles, rolled
in the snow, leaped up
to touch my arms with her nose.

Dizzy, I stopped turning, stood still.

Angus was dancing, his swollen feet
just barely fitting into his boots, shoelaces
untied and flapping, his arms flying
                         like a ballet dancer.
Like a farmer who's taken up ballet.

Mum danced. I danced. All of us
in the snow, the bitter cold, under the stars,
danced beneath the northern lights.

Author's Note

Not so long ago — say, thirty years ago — not much was known about mental disorders. Doctors and nurses did their best, but few medications for brain illnesses existed. Treatments were tried that often did more harm than good.

Today doctors and researchers know a great deal more about the brain. It is now widely understood that a mental illness is like any other illness of the body. To have anxiety or obsessive-compulsive disorder, for example, is like having asthma or a heart condition. Better medicines are now available, and most people with brain illnesses live normal lives.

The Crazy Man is a work of fiction. Any references to actual events and locales, and any references or resemblances to persons living or dead are used for the purpose of fiction and are entirely coincidental. I would like to thank James Porter and Rob Porter for sharing their vast knowledge of farming, and particularly of farming techniques in the 1960s; I am also grateful to them for their recollections of growing up in a town that was also home to the Saskatchewan Hospital.

In addition, I wish to thank Jean, Janet and Kathy

Porter for the many times they chatted together about their prairie years when they perhaps forgot I was listening. Thank you also to Shelley Tanaka, my editor, for her keen eye and ear. Grateful acknowledgment goes to the Canada Council for the Arts for its support of the creation of this work. And finally, to Meeka — I heard you found a good home, and I'm glad.

Poet and novelist PAMELA PORTER was born in Albuquerque, New Mexico. She lived in New Mexico, Texas, Louisiana, Washington and Montana before immigrating to Canada with her husband, the fourth generation of a Saskatchewan farming family. *The Crazy Man* was inspired by stories she heard from her husband's family, who still have a farm near Weyburn, Saskatchewan, where Pamela spends part of every year.

Pamela Porter is the author of a children's novel, *Sky*, and her poetry has appeared in literary magazines in Canada and the U.S. She now lives with her family in Sidney, B.C.